Silly Jack

Holly Surplice

For Rory,
Daisy and Monroe

First published 2006 by Walker Books Ltd
87 Vauxhall Walk, London SE11 5HJ
2 4 6 8 10 9 7 5 3 1 ©2006 Holly Surplice
The moral right of Holly Surplice to be identified as the author and illustrator of this work
has been asserted by her in accordance with the Copyright, Designs and Patents Act 1988.
This book has been typeset in Jacobs-Rubberstamp. Printed in China. All rights reserved. No part of this book may be reproduced,
transmitted or stored in an information retrieval system in any form or by any means, graphic, electronic or mechanical, including photocopying, taping and recording,
without prior written permission from the publisher. British Library Cataloguing in Publication Data: a catalogue record for this book is available
from the British Library ISBN-13: 978-1-4063-0304-9 (HB); 978-0-7445-5768-8 (PB) ISBN-10: 1-4063-0304-6 (HB); 0-7445-5768-2 (PB) www.walkerbooks.co.uk

WALKER BOOKS
AND SUBSIDIARIES
LONDON · BOSTON · SYDNEY · AUCKLAND

Jack has just arrived at his new home, Moss Farm.
There are lots of new friends
to meet ...

Juniper the goat, Dilly the dog,
Clarissa, Lilly and Rose the chickens,
Camilla the cow, Tiger the cat,
Albert and Elizabeth
the geese.

"Neigh!" says Jack.

"I'm Jack the..."

But Jack does not know
what kind of animal he is.

"Am I a **COW?**"

neighs Jack.

Jack eats grass like a cow,
but he cannot stick
his tongue right up
his nose like
Camilla can.

"CAT ... or a DOG!"

neighs Jack.

Jack prowls like Tiger
and gets dizzy
like Dilly.

Woof! Woof! Woof!

Purrr! Purrr!

"Silly Jack!"
Tiger and Dilly
purr and bark.
"You are not
a cat or a dog.
You are a – "

"CHICKEN!"

neighs Jack.

Jack perches like a chicken,

but Jack cannot lay even the tiniest egg.

Cluck! Cluck! Cluck!

"Silly Jack!" clucks Clarissa. "You are not a chicken, you are a – "

"GOAT!"

neighs Jack.

Jack and Juniper
eat socks that have
been hung out to dry.

"Silly Jack!"

bleats Juniper.
"You are not a goat,
you are a – "

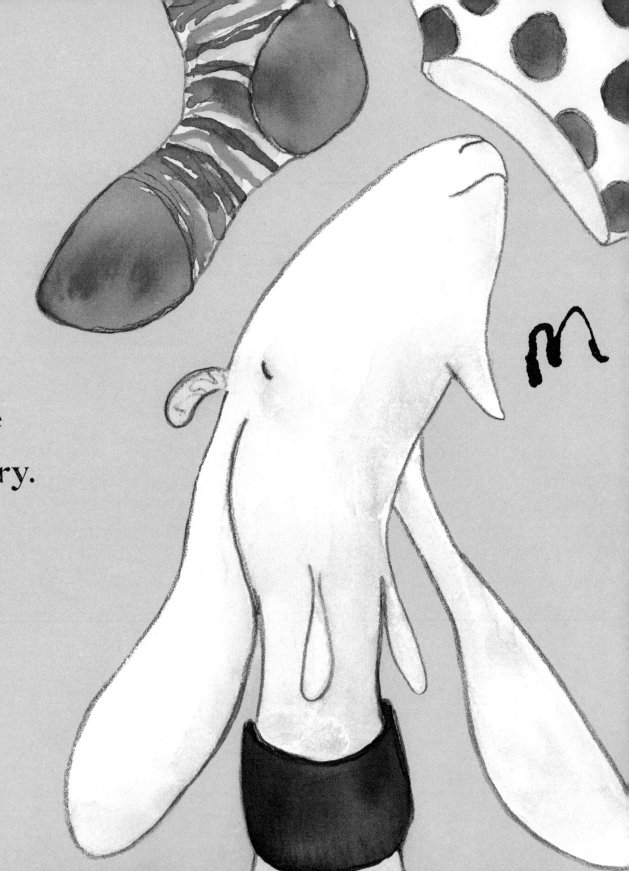

"GOOSE!"

neighs Jack.

Jack gets chased by the geese!

"Silly Jack!"
honks Albert.
"You are not a goose,

you are a – "

honk

honk

honk

honk honk

"HORSE!"

the animals

moo

and bleat

and bark

and honk

and purr

and cluck.

"A HORSE!
Of course!"
neighs Jack.

neigh!

neigh!

neigh!

"I can
jump!

And I can
buck!

I can
swish!

And I can
chase!

neigh!

I can gallop faster than **anyone!**

I love being a horse!"

And everyone loves

JACK!